For Elvira and Mel

C.M.

First published in 2005 in Great Britain by
Gullane Children's Books
an imprint of Pinwheel Limited
Winchester House, 259-269 Old Marylebone Road,
London NW1 5XJ

1 3 5 7 9 10 8 6 4 2

A CIP record for this title is available from the British Library.

ISBN 1-86233-571-0 hardback

Printed and bound in Singapore

NOT OLD ENOUGH

Charlotte Middleton

GULLANE™
CHILDREN'S BOOKS

It was almost
Eva's birthday.
But she was feeling fed up of being
the smallest and the youngest in her family.

She could NEVER reach the biscuits . . .

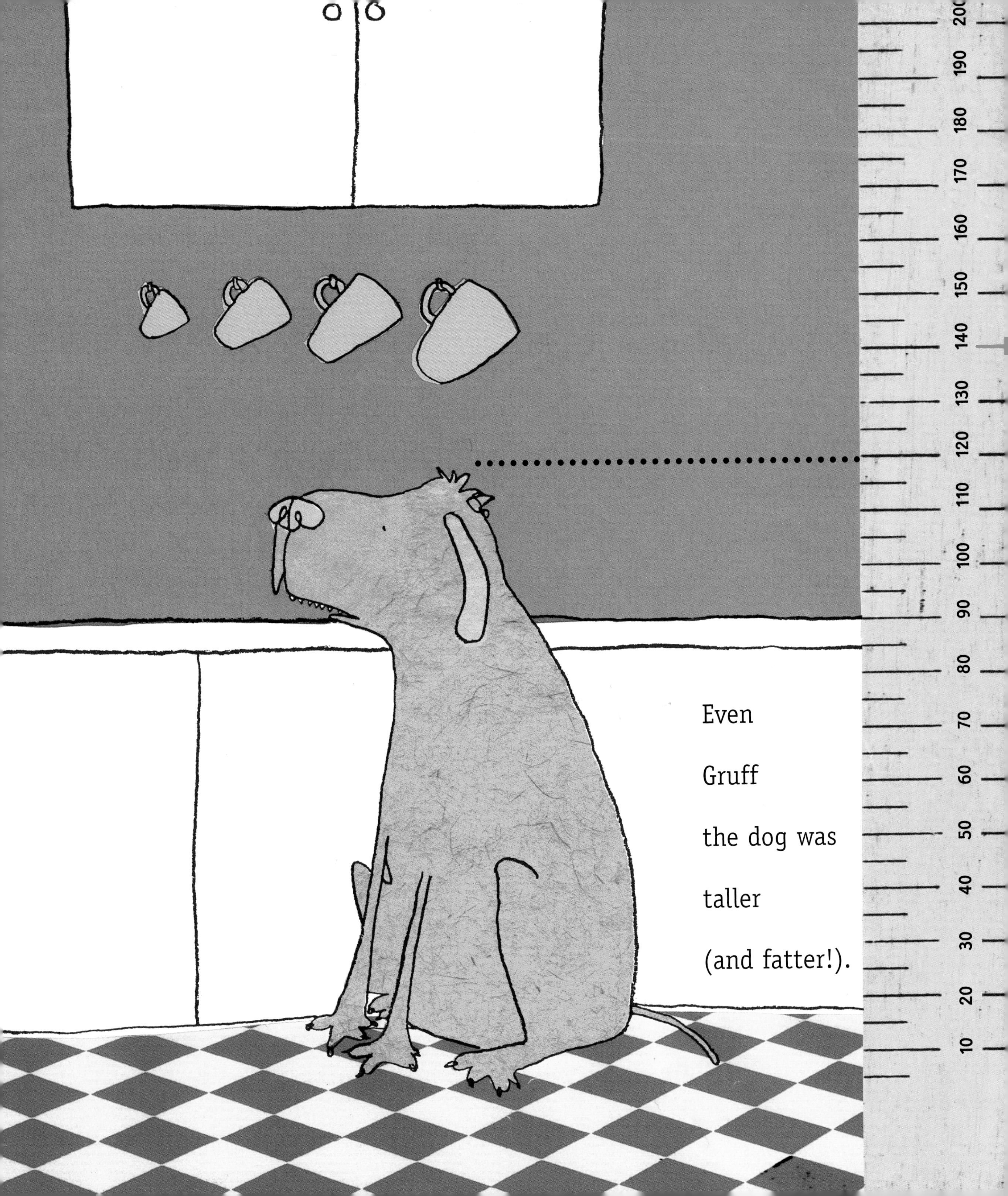
Even
Gruff
the dog was
taller
(and fatter!).
10
20
30
40
50
60
70
80
90
100
110
120
130
140
150
160
170
180
190
200

She always had to
stand in goal because
Billy said she was
too small to kick
the ball properly . . .

she *always*
had to go to bed
the earliest . . .

. . . and she wasn't allowed the pretty pink pointy shoes she'd seen in the shop.

Her mummy always said "Sorry, Eva, you're just not old enough . . ."

The day before her birthday,
Eva decided to put on her
mummy's things to make
herself look really grown up . . .

but Billy laughed
and said she looked
"absolutely
RIDICULOUS!"

. . . well, that was the **final straw!**

Eva decided she would show her family that she was old enough to do whatever she wanted! So she packed her things and moved out . . .

to the *very* end
of the back garden!

She set up her own new home . . . (well, eventually!)

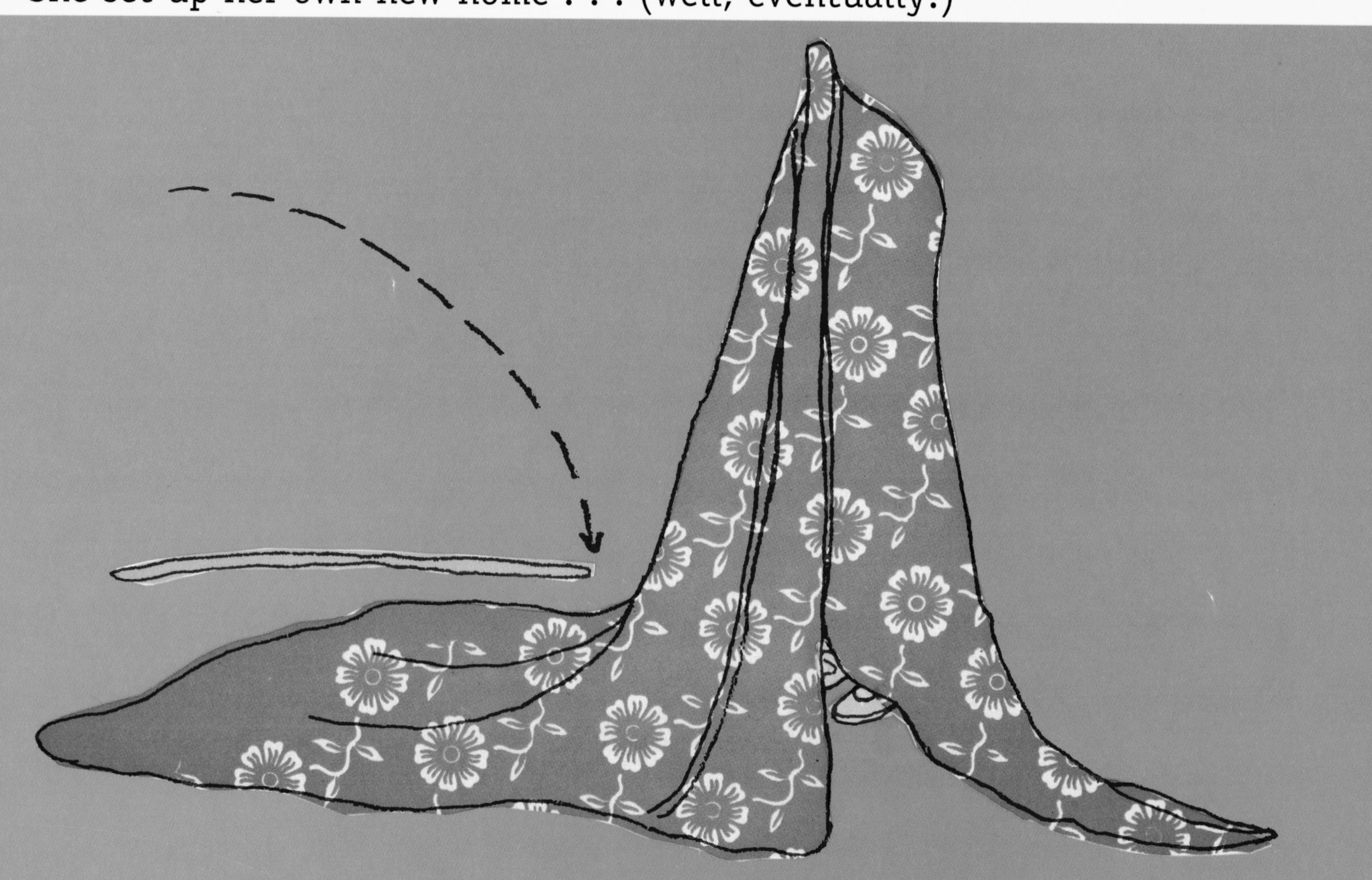

and she felt really grown-up.

She planned to get a job.
Probably as an **extremely famous**
clothes designer . . .

and she planned
to buy **pointy** shoes
and wear **bright pink** lipstick
and **everyone** would
admire her!

After Eva had finished planning her
new grown-up life, it felt very late.
So she decided to go to bed.

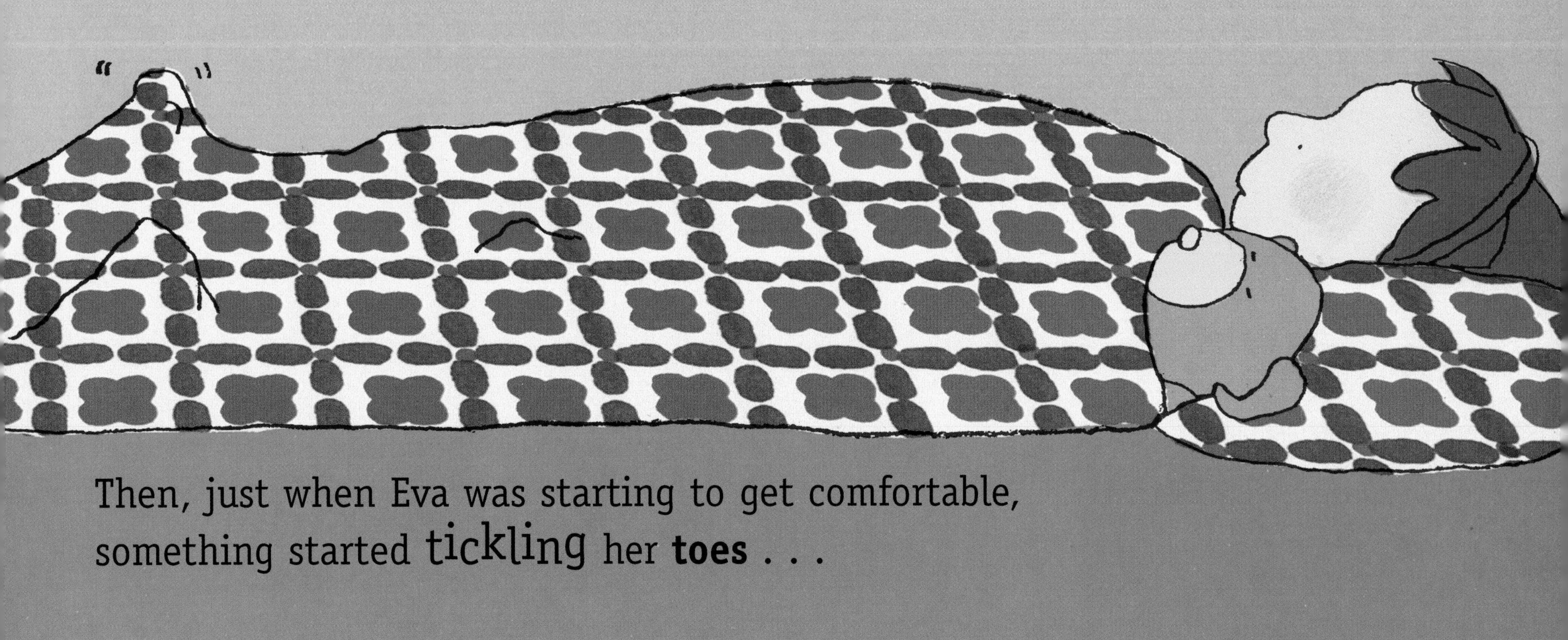

Then, just when Eva was starting to get comfortable,
something started tickling her **toes** . . .

and then it tickled her **fingers** . . .

and **then** . . .

Aaagh!

It was the

BIGGEST,

hairiest,

spider

in the whole *world* . . .

. . . **and** it was
on Eva's nose!

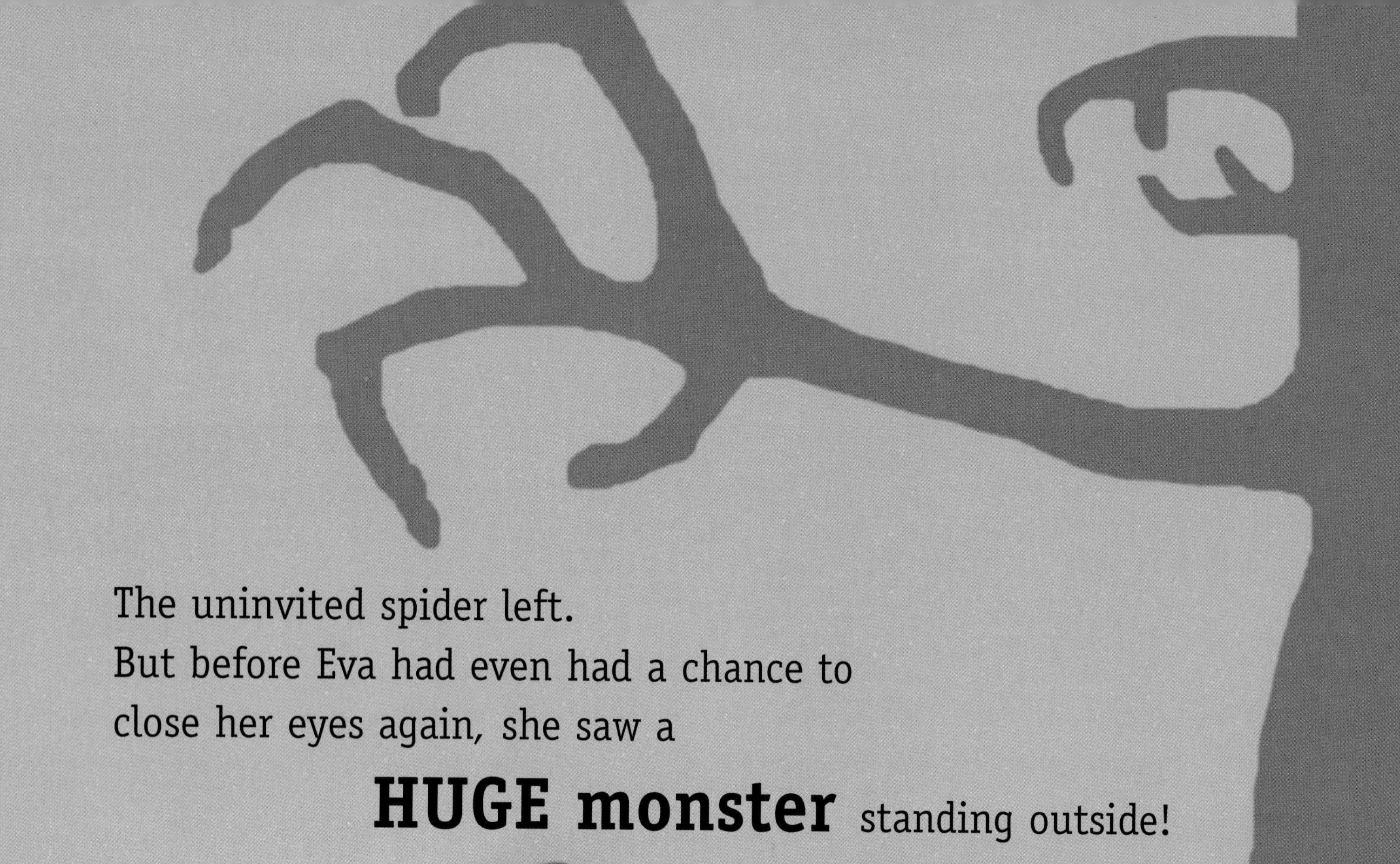

The uninvited spider left.
But before Eva had even had a chance to
close her eyes again, she saw a

HUGE monster standing outside!

Now that Eva was a grown-up
she felt she had no choice but to
have a stern word with the monster
(even though this would be very scary) . . .

Luckily, it wasn't a monster after all!

Eva felt really quite tired now, and a bit lonely. . .
and it was very hard to sleep
on two bumpy rocks
that wouldn't budge!

Being a grown-up was not so fun anymore. And just when Eva's tummy was starting to rumble ever so loudly, she heard something else . . .

There was a rustling and a snuffling sound . . . and it was getting closer and **closer!**

It was Gruff and Billy!

Eva had to admit – she was more than a tiny bit pleased to see them.

"There you are!" said Billy. "Please come back to the house for supper – we've been worried about you!"

Eva was really glad that Billy and Gruff had come to find her! *Perhaps,* she thought, *being the youngest isn't so bad after all . . .*

And for her birthday the next day,
Eva got the best present EVER from
Mummy and Billy . . .

It was a new pair of **pink, sparkly** shoes (with bows)!!
Eva **loved** them! They made her feel grown-up,
and very special indeed.